Robin Hill School

The Luck of
the Irish

For the Cousins
—M.M.

ALADDIN PAPERBACKS
An imprint of Simon & Schuster Children's Publishing Division
1230 Avenue of the Americas, New York, NY 10020
Text copyright © 2007 by Brenda Bowen
Illustrations copyright © 2007 by Mike Gordon
Color by Carl Gordon
READY-TO-READ is a registered trademark of Simon & Schuster, Inc.
ALADDIN PAPERBACKS and colophon are trademarks of Simon & Schuster, Inc.
Designed by Sammy Yuen Jr.
The text of this book was set in Century Schoolbook.
Manufactured in the United States of America
First Aladdin Paperbacks edition January 2007
2 4 6 8 10 9 7 5 3 1
Library of Congress Cataloging-in-Publication Data
McNamara, Margaret.
The luck of the Irish / by Margaret McNamara ; illustrated by Mike Gordon.
—1st Aladdin Paperbacks ed.
p. cm.—(Robin Hill School) (Ready-to-read)
Summary: Katie and her family make shamrocks for each of her
classmates to celebrate St. Patrick's Day, but when Mrs. Connor
shows a shamrock that looks very different, Katie is sad until, together,
they learn the distinction between a shamrock and a four-leaf clover.
[1. Clover—Fiction. 2. Saint Patrick's Day—Fiction. 3. Schools —Fiction.
4. Irish Americans—Fiction.]   I. Gordon, Mike, ill.
II. Title. III. Series: McNamara, Margaret. Robin Hill School.
IV. Series: Ready-to-read.
PZ7.M232518Luc 2007
[E]—dc22   2006008196
ISBN-13: 978-1-4169-1539-3 (pbk.)
ISBN-10: 1-4169-1539-7 (pbk.)
ISBN-13: 978-1-4169-1540-9 (library ed.)
ISBN-10: 1-4169-1540-0 (library ed.)

The Luck of
the Irish

Written by Margaret McNamara
Illustrated by Mike Gordon

Ready-to-Read

Aladdin

New York   London   Toronto   Sydney

On March 16,
at Robin Hill School,
Mrs. Connor said,
"Tomorrow is
Saint Patrick's Day."

"Saint Patrick
lived in Ireland
long ago,"
she told the class.

"My family is
from Ireland," said Katie.
"Then you have
the luck of the Irish,"
said Mrs. Connor.

That night,
Katie and her family
made a shamrock
for every first-grader
in Katie's class.

"Shamrocks have
three leaves,"
said Katie's mother.
"And the leaves
are shaped like hearts."

"Are shamrocks Irish?"
asked Katie.

"They are," said her father.

The next day Mrs. Connor
wore a green skirt
and a green sweater.
"Happy Saint Patrick's Day!"
she said.

She took something
out of her bag.

It was big.

It was green.

It had four leaves,
and they were not shaped
like hearts.

"Do you know what this is?"
she asked.

"A shamrock!" said Michael.

"Right!" said Mrs. Connor.

All that day, Katie
did not feel very lucky.

Mrs. Connor noticed.
"Why are you so sad
on Saint Patrick's Day?"
she asked.

21

Katie showed Mrs. Connor
the shamrocks
she had made
for the class.

Mrs. Connor looked at them carefully.

"Your shamrocks are
different than mine,"
she said.
Katie nodded.

"I think we should find out
more about shamrocks,"
said Mrs. Connor.

She took a book
off the shelf.

The book showed a shamrock.
It looked just like Katie's.

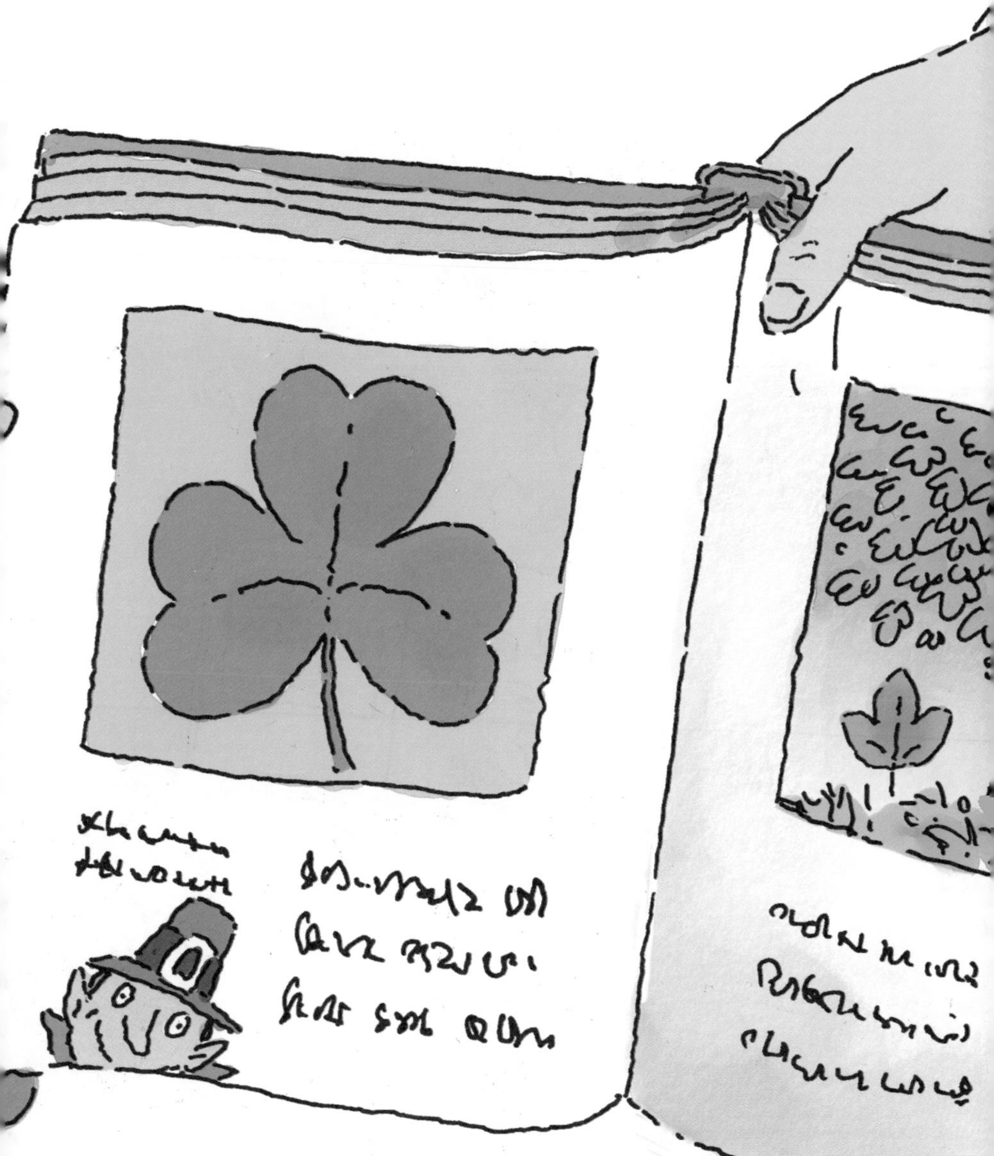

The book also showed a
four-leaf clover.

It looked just like
Mrs. Connor's.
"Katie," said Mrs. Connor,
"you learn something new
every day."

"If you are lucky,"
said Katie.